Good Knight, MUSTACHE BABY

BRIDGET HEOS *Illustrations by* **JOY ANG**

CLARION BOOKS | Houghton Mifflin Harcourt | Boston New York

Clarion Books
3 Park Avenue
New York, New York 10016

Clarion Books is an imprint of Houghton Mifflin Harcourt Publishing Company.

hmhbooks.com

The illustrations in this book were executed digitally.
The text was set in Tweed SG.
Cover design by Phil Caminiti
Interior design by Phil Caminiti

Note: The motto *Hirtis Fortuna Favet* on the back cover is Latin for "Fortune Favors the Hairy Ones."

Library of Congress Cataloging-in-Publication Data is available.
ISBN 978-0-358-43468-9

Manufactured in China
SCP 10 9 8 7 6 5 4 3 2 1
4500830168

For Johnny, Richie, J.J., and Sami Jeanne
—B.H.

To Carissa H.
—J.A.

Once upon a time, there lived two brave knights:

Baby Billy, House of Mustache,
and Baby Javier, House of Beard.

United in friendship, they spent their days

riding,

jousting,

and slaying giants.

Yet each night,
darkness befell them.

By law of the land, feasting, fighting, and fun ended at the stroke of seven.

At that hour, all babies
were banished to bedtime.

From their towers, Billy and Javier could hear the laughter of their brothers and sisters below.

This injustice would not stand! They vowed to conquer bedtime, once and for all.

The next night, the babies suited up
and rode out to a festival.

There were contests,
crafts, and . . .

. . . a secret meeting of the

KNIGHTS OF THE ROUND TABLE.

It was decided: at festival's end, the young knights would rebel. There would be no bedtime tonight!

Soon, a storyteller arrived to great fanfare.

"Once upon a time..."
She spun a tale of ogres,
giants, trolls, and dragons.

It was frightening enough to make Billy's hair curl.
Yet he listened steadfastly.

At the turn of the final page,
Sir Billy signaled the troops.

CHARGE!

But where were the other knights?

Alas, the storybook was enchanted.
Sir Javier and the others had fallen under its spell.

All save Billy.

He fought valiantly, but in the end he was captured by the lord and lady of the House of Mustache . . .

. . . and banished to the castle turret.

Sir Billy vowed to escape. Bedtime be dashed.

He climbed down the castle wall

only to splash into a menacing moat.

As fate would have it, a goodly beast
rescued him and carried him
through an enchanted forest.

Sadly, he was caught
once beyond the woods,

a second time
rappelling down the cliffs,

and a third time
sailing across the sea.

Never losing heart, he made it ever farther
until at last he reached the Sea of Hot Lava.

Freedom lay on its distant shores.

But as he leapt
from island to island,
he was captured by
two meddling trolls

and brought to
the lord and lady
of the house.

The lord and lady were angered by his escape
but sympathetic to his plight.

In the end, they met his every demand:
water, a hanky, and even a story.

THE story.
They must have borrowed it from the storyteller!
Billy listened wholeheartedly, forgetting it was enchanted.
Spellbound, his eyes grew ever so heavy.

But Billy never surrendered.

He remained ever
poised and alert.

In the end, he conquered bedtime . . .

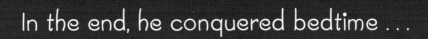

...and became a **LEGEND**.

Billy rescued Javier
and, together . . .

...they performed heroic deeds throughout the land.

Time went by,

and their mustache and beard grew

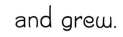
and grew.

Yet, somehow, they made it home in time . . .

. . . for beard-fast.